Kipper's Monster

Mick Inkpen

Hodder
Children's
Books

A division of Hodder Headline Limited

Tiger had a brand new torch.
'It's the most powerful torch there is!' he said to Kipper.
He shone it at Big Owl.
He shone it at Hippo.
He shone it in Kipper's face.
'You should see it when it's dark!' he said. 'It's REALLY good when it's dark!'

Other Kipper books

WHERE, OH WHERE, IS KIPPER'S BEAR?
KIPPER
KIPPER'S TOYBOX
KIPPER'S BIRTHDAY
KIPPER'S SNOWY DAY
KIPPER'S CHRISTMAS EVE
KIPPER AND ROLY
KIPPER'S BOOK OF COLOUR
KIPPER'S BOOK OF WEATHER
KIPPER'S BOOK OF COUNTING
KIPPER'S BOOK OF OPPOSITES
THE LITTLE KIPPERS
KIPPER STORY COLLECTION
LITTLE KIPPER STORY COLLECTION
KIPPER'S A TO Z

First published 2002
by Hodder Children's Books,
a division of Hodder Headline Limited,
338 Euston Road, London NW1 3BH

Copyright © Mick Inkpen 2002

10 9 8 7 6 5 4 3 2 1

ISBN 0340841761 HB

A catalogue record for this book is
available from the British Library.
The right of Mick Inkpen to be identified
as the author of this Work
has been asserted by him
in accordance with the
Copyright, Designs and
Patents Act 1988

Printed in Hong Kong

He sat in Kipper's basket and pulled the blanket over his head.

'Come on! We can make it dark under here!' he said.

Under the blanket was one of Kipper's storybooks.

'That's another thing!' said Tiger. 'You can read under the bedclothes with a torch like this!'

Kipper began to read.
'Deep in the middle of the dark, dark wood, there lived a horrible, horrendous, terrible, tremendous . . .'

'That's it!' shouted Tiger, jumping up. 'We'll camp in the woods tonight! It'll be really, REALLY dark in the woods.'

'Shall I bring my book?' said Kipper.

So they took the book, and
some biscuits, and they put up
their tent in the middle of the woods,
at the bottom of Big Hill.

But as it began to get dark
Tiger began to think that perhaps
it wasn't such a good idea after all.

'Come inside and have a
biscuit,' said Kipper. 'Do you
want Rabbit or
Big Owl?'

B ut Tiger didn't reply. He was
looking nervously out of the door.
'Do you think there are any bears
in these woods?' he whispered.

'No, I shouldn't think so,' said Kipper. He began to read.

'Deep in the middle of the dark, dark wood, there lived a horrible. . .'

But Tiger wasn't ready. He asked Kipper to sit next to the door, instead of him. And when Kipper tried again to read, Tiger got up and zipped the door shut altogether.

But the third time Kipper tried
to read, from somewhere
outside the tent, there came the
most terrible, tremendous, horrible,
horrendous,

'Screech!'

'What was that?' said Kipper.
Tiger said nothing.

'Let's go and look!' whispered
Kipper. So they crept out of the tent
and into the woods, shining Tiger's
torch ahead of them.

'I think it came from somewhere
near here,' said Kipper. The torch
beam lit up the enormous, grey
trunk of an old tree.

There in the middle was
a dark, dark hole.

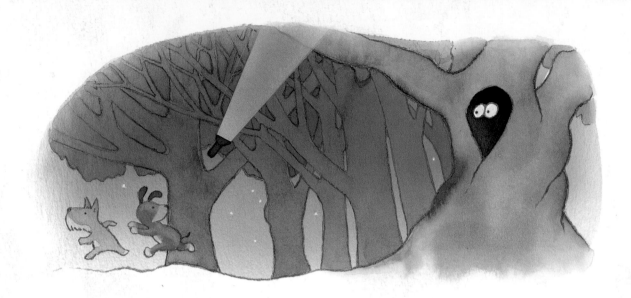

Suddenly a huge pair of
yellow eyes blinked open, and
from the hole came the most terrible,

'Screech!'

They shrieked and ran, bumping
into each other and sending the
torch flying. They scrambled into the
tent and lay there panting hard,
listening. . .

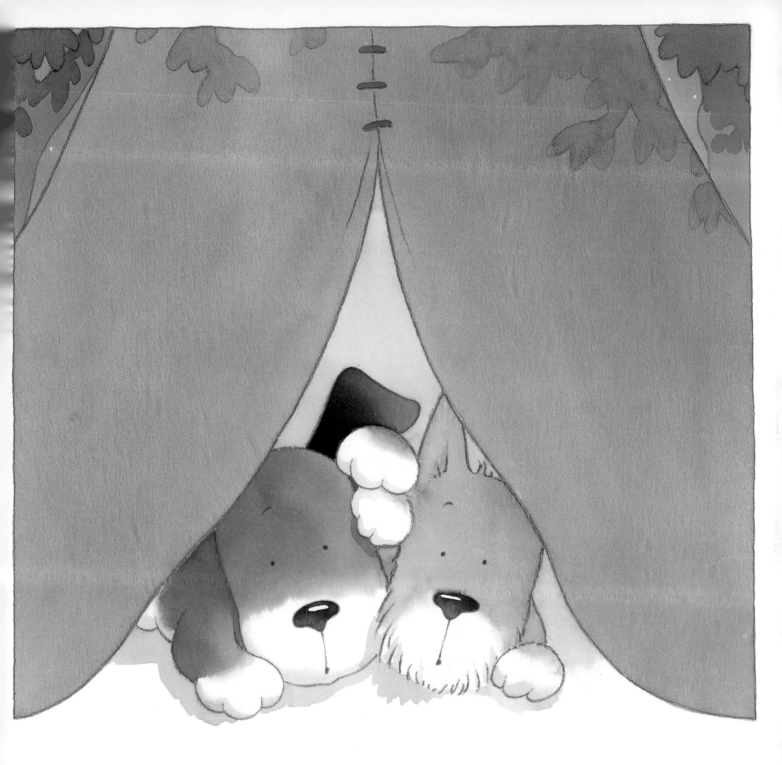

'I think it was just an owl,' whispered Kipper. 'Yes, it was just a silly, old owl.'

But behind him, the shadow of something was growing on the wall of the tent.

Something with horns.

'It's a horrible, horrendous monster!' squealed Tiger.

The shape on the tent, grew and grew till it was looming above them. Then it slowly changed into a shape that Kipper had seen before.

Kipper crept back out of the tent and walked towards the torchlight. There, caught in the beam, was a little snail.

Kipper picked up the torch and let the snail crawl onto his paw. He looked at the snail closely.

Its horns curled in and out as he touched them.

'I've found the horrible, horrendous monster! Look Tiger!'

Tiger peeped out from underneath the blanket.

He saw the snail.

He saw its shadow.

He felt silly.

'Shall I read the story now?'
said Kipper.

But Kipper never did get to read his story, because they went home to Tiger's house, where they put up the tent in Tiger's bedroom. . .

. . .and Tiger got to read it instead.